WHITE WATER
WIPE OUT!

ROGER HURN
Illustrated by **LUKE FINLAYSON**

TITLES AT THIS LEVEL

Fiction

STUNT **RIDERS**
DAVID and HELEN ORME
978 1 4451 1314 2 pb

UNARMED AND **DANGEROUS**
DAVID and HELEN ORME
978 1 4451 1316 6 pb

WALK INTO **DANGER**
DAVID and HELEN ORME
978 1 4451 1318 0 pb

ROBBED!
ANNE CASSIDY
978 1 4451 1815 4 pb

WOLFHOLD
STEVE BARLOW and STEVE SKIDMORE
978 1 4451 1814 7 pb

WHITE WATER **WIPE OUT!**
ROGER HURN
978 1 4451 1816 1 pb

Graphic fiction

ALIEN **CAGE**
JONNY ZUCKER
978 1 4451 1322 7 pb

FUTURE **TENSE**
JONNY ZUCKER and LEE CARTER
978 1 4451 1320 3 pb

THE **DECIDERS**
JONNY ZUCKER and ANDREW FIJN
978 1 4451 1324 1 pb

ASSASSIN **CITY**
JONNY ZUCKER and PEDRO J. COLOMBO
978 1 4451 1803 1 pb

SWORD OF **LEGEND**
JONNY ZUCKER and CENARO WHITE
978 1 4451 1802 4 pb

SWITCH **FACE**
JONNY ZUCKER and REV HONGDO
978 1 4451 1804 8 pb

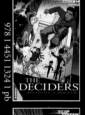

Non-fiction

SUPER **ANIMALS**
ANNE ROONEY
978 1 4451 1358 6 pb

WORLD'S **FASTEST**
ANNE ROONEY
978 1 4451 1360 9 pb

GREATEST ROCK **BANDS**
ANNE ROONEY
978 1 4451 1310 4 hb
978 1 4451 1359 3 pb

SPACE
ANNE ROONEY
978 1 4451 1956 4 hb

DARING **ESCAPES**
ANNE ROONEY
978 1 4451 1957 1 hb

HOW TO SPEND **A BILLION**
ANNE ROONEY
978 1 4451 1955 7 hb

SLIP STREAM

WHITE WATER WIPE OUT!

ROGER HURN
Illustrated by **LUKE FINLAYSON**

EDGE
FRANKLIN WATTS

LONDON•SYDNEY

First published in 2013 by
Franklin Watts
338 Euston Road
London NW1 3BH

Franklin Watts Australia
Level 17/207 Kent Street
Sydney NSW 2000

Text © Roger Hurn 2013
Illustration © Franklin Watts 2013

A CIP catalogue record for this book is
available from the British Library.

(ebook) ISBN: 978 1 4451 1822 2
(pb) ISBN: 978 1 4451 1816 1
(library ebook) ISBN: 978 1 4451 2608 1

Series Editors: Adrian Cole and Jackie Hamley
Series Advisors: Diana Bentley and Dee Reid
Series Designer: Peter Scoulding

1 3 5 7 9 10 8 6 4 2

Printed in China

Franklin Watts is a division of
Hachette Children's Books,
an Hachette UK company.
www.hachette.co.uk

CONTENTS

CHAPTER 1
WHITE WATER

Rick and Ali's class were on a school trip.

They went white water rafting.

"That was awesome!" shouted Ali.

"I was SO much better than you!" yelled Rick.

"You're joking! You nearly wiped out,"

said Ali.

"Hey, look at that run up there!" said Rick.

"That's the Hell Hole," said Mr Brown. "It's off limits to all of you. It's too dangerous for beginners!"

"Says who?" whispered Rick.

"Don't even think about it!" said Ali.

"Is that a challenge?" Rick laughed.

CHAPTER 2

MISSING!

That night, Ali woke up. He saw Rick's bed.

It was empty and his jacket was missing.

"Idiot," he thought. "He's going to try the

Hell Hole. I know he is."

Ali raced to the boat house. Rick was already in a kayak, heading towards the Hell Hole. "Stop!" yelled Ali. But he was too late. He ran down the riverbank.

The water was too wild and Rick's kayak capsized.

Rick surfaced but he was soon swept away.

Ali looked around for any way to help.

CHAPTER 3
HELP ME!

Ali grabbed a throw bag and raced along the

riverbank. Rick was nearly at the Hell Hole.

Ali held one end of the rope from the throw bag.

He took aim and threw the bag to Rick.

Rick grabbed the bag. But the water was

so fast that he pulled Ali over.

Ali slid along the riverbank.

If he fell in, they would both drown.

CHAPTER 4
WIPE OUT?

Ali saw a small tree on the riverbank.

He grasped at it with one hand.

The tree bent but it stopped his fall.

Ali wound the rope around the tree.

Slowly, Ali pulled Rick back towards the riverbank.

At last Rick scrambled onto the bank.

"Thanks Ali," he gasped.

"You nearly wiped us BOTH out that time,"

laughed Ali.

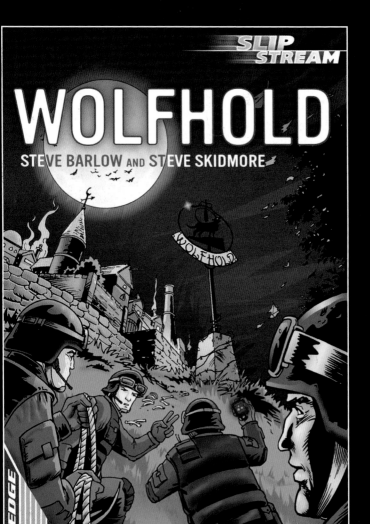

Tom wakes up in a strange house, in a strange place.
There are no phones, papers or internet, and no way out.

Where is he? And how did he get there? Can the mysterious
Megan help him remember and solve the mystery?

LONDON·SYDNEY

ROBBED!

ANNE CASSIDY

CASH POINT

EDGE

Tommy is late and his sister Lizzie is worried. She is told
that Big Alex is taking him to the cash machine.

Lizzie is sure that Tommy is about to be robbed.
What can she do?

LONDON•SYDNEY

About SLIPSTREAM

Slipstream is a series of expertly levelled books designed for pupils who are struggling with reading. Its unique three-strand approach through fiction, graphic fiction and non-fiction gives pupils a rich reading experience that will accelerate their progress and close the reading gap.

At the heart of every Slipstream fiction book is a great story. Easily accessible words and phrases ensure that pupils both decode and comprehend, and the high interest stories really engage older struggling readers.

Whether you're using Slipstream Level 1 for Guided Reading or as an independent read, here are some suggestions:

1. Make each reading session successful. Talk about the text before the pupil starts reading. Introduce any unfamiliar vocabulary.

2. Encourage the pupil to talk about the book using a range of open questions. For example, would they like to try an extreme sport?

3. Discuss the differences between reading fiction, graphic fiction and non-fiction.

Slipstream Level 1 photocopiable **WORKBOOK**
ISBN: 978 1 4451 1798 0
available – download free sample worksheets from:
www.franklinwatts.co.uk

For guidance, SLIPSTREAM Level 1 – White Water Wipe Out! has been approximately measured to:

National Curriculum Level: 2c
Reading Age: 7.0–7.6
Book Band: Turquoise

ATOS: 1.8*
Guided Reading Level: H
Lexile® Measure (confirmed): 340L

*Please check actual Accelerated Reader™ book level and quiz availability at www.arbookfind.co.uk